Groundwood Books / House of Anansi Press
110 Spadina Avenue, Suite 801, Toronto, Ontario M5V 2K4
or c/o Publishers Group West
1700 Fourth Street, Berkeley, CA 94710

We acknowledge for their financial support of our publishing program
the Canada Council for the Arts, the Government of Canada through
the Canada Book Fund (CBF) and the Ontario Arts Council.

Canada Council   Conseil des Arts   ONTARIO ARTS COUNCIL
for the Arts   du Canada   CONSEIL DES ARTS DE L'ONTARIO

Library and Archives Canada Cataloguing in Publication

Trottier, Maxine
Migrant / Maxine Trottier ; Isabelle Arsenault, illustrator.

ISBN 978-0-88899-975-7

1. Mennonites — Canada — Juvenile fiction. 2. Mennonites —
Mexico — Juvenile fiction. 3. Migrant agricultural laborers —
Canada — Juvenile fiction. I. Arsenault, Isabelle II. Title.

PS8589.R685M54 2011   jC813'.54   C2010-903436-8

Design by Michael Solomon
The illustrations were rendered in mixed media — watercolor, gouache,
crayons and collage.
Printed and bound in China

For Donna Logan. — MT

To my sister, Hélène. — IA

ACKNOWLEDGMENTS
My appreciation to
Dr. Doreen Helen Klassen
for her insights. — MT

MIGRANT

Maxine Trottier

PICTURES BY
Isabelle Arsenault

GROUNDWOOD BOOKS
HOUSE OF ANANSI PRESS
TORONTO   BERKELEY

THERE ARE TIMES when Anna feels like a bird.
It is the birds, after all, that fly north in the
spring and south every fall, chasing the sun,
following the warmth.

Her family is a flock of geese beating its way
there and back again.

What would it be like to stay in one place — to have your own bed, to ride your own bicycle? Anna wonders.
Now that would be something.

There are moments when she feels like a rabbit. Not the sort with the white fluff of tail, but a jack rabbit. Those rabbits live in abandoned burrows, her father has told her.

When her mother works hard to make a home of yet another empty farmhouse, the rooms filled with the ghosts of last year's workers, Anna feels like a jack rabbit.

A bee. That is what she is during the day. Not a worker bee, though.

Anna is too young to work. But when no one is watching, she picks a tomato now and again. Just the small ones.

When her parents' backs are bent under the hot sun, when her older brothers and sisters dip and rise, dip and rise over the vegetables, that is when all of them are bees.

At night Anna is a kitten sharing a bed with her sisters, all of them under one blanket when the nights are cool.
A kitten is a good thing to be, a safe thing, curled there with your sisters by your side.

In the other room her brothers are like puppies, growling and nipping in their sleep, fighting over a blanket that barely covers them all.

When they shop for groceries at the cheap store, Anna is shy because people often stare.

She listens to all the voices — to the woman with pink hair at the cash register, to the tattooed men who put cans on the shelves. But she only understands some of their words. Dollars. Peas. Meatballs.

A few people talk the way she does, the good plain German rolling off their tongues as sweetly as sugar. Others chatter together, their words as spicy as the hottest chilis, or as slow and rich as dark molasses.

To Anna's ears, it is as though a thousand crickets are all singing a different song.

What would it be like to be a tree with roots sunk deeply into the earth — to watch the seasons passing around you the same way the wind passes through your branches?

When fall came and your leaves fell, they
would blow away, but you would remain.
   You'd watch black and orange butterflies
set out in wobbly flight, feel the days grow
shorter, look up in the sky and see a line of
geese winging south yet again.

And then you would sleep, wrapped in
snow, until the sky-high honking of geese
woke you in the spring.
    Now that would be something.

But fall is here, and the geese are flying away.

And with them goes Anna, like a monarch, like a robin, like a feather in the wind.

CANADA AND THE UNITED STATES were built by people who valued freedom and opportunity. That is part of the reason so many came to North America in search of a fresh beginning in spite of the challenges. A different language often had to be learned. Old customs were replaced by new ones. Success was not guaranteed, and acceptance sometimes came slowly. Even today, people willingly make sacrifices to live in a place where respect is extended to both citizens and visitors.

Some of those visitors are seasonal laborers, or migrants. They come to Canada and the United States without their families to work, and then must return to their home country. But one special group of migrants – Mennonites from Mexico – kept their Canadian citizenship when they moved to Mexico in the 1920s. There they hoped to farm, withdraw from the modern world and find religious freedom. But